The Wiggles

FUNTASTIC STORYTIME COLLECTION™

Designed by David Ciro

Illustrated by Paul E. Nunn

funtastic™

First published in Australia by Funtastic Limited, 2005
800 Wellington Road, Rowville, Victoria 3178, Australia
Ph: 61 3 9213 0100 Fax: 61 3 9213 0199
www.funtastic.com.au Email: publishing@funtastic.com.au

Printed and bound in China

The Wiggles woke up very early one morning.

'With all the concerts we've had lately, we haven't been sleeping enough,' said Jeff.

The Wiggles laughed and shook their heads.

Anthony said, 'But you're always sleeping, Jeff!'

Jeff shrugged. 'Lately, we have been singing, travelling, cooking, cleaning, and ...'

Murray yawned again. 'Jeff does have a point. We haven't been getting enough rest.'

Anthony was hungry. He reached for a box of raisins that he had left on the table the night before.

'I was sure I left a box of raisins on the table. But now it's gone!' Anthony said, yawning.

Greg rubbed his eyes. 'That's funny. I was sure my magic hat was on the bookshelf. But now it's on the hat rack.'

Murray stretched. 'That's the second time this week your hat has moved!'

'Look at my jigsaw puzzle!' Jeff exclaimed. 'I'm sure I didn't have all those clouds put together yet. Someone's been putting together my puzzle.'

The Wiggles knew that something strange was going on. They wondered who could be doing all of this. It must be happening while they were asleep. They decided to make a plan.

So that night, instead of crawling into their cozy beds, The Wiggles tried to stay awake. Anthony made a sandwich. Murray composed a song. Greg practised his magic tricks, and Jeff worked on his jigsaw puzzle.

But, one by one, The Wiggles dropped off to dreamland. Jeff fell asleep right on his puzzle. Anthony nodded off on top of his sandwich! Murray dozed through the last verse of his lullaby. Greg closed his eyes just as the bunny was finally going to pop out of his magic hat.

The next morning, The Wiggles woke up.
'I don't even remember falling asleep,' Anthony said.
'One minute I was about to sink my teeth into a sandwich and the next ...'
'We must've all fallen asleep!' Murray exclaimed. 'Is anything missing?'

'My loaf of bread is gone!" Anthony exclaimed. He looked in the refrigerator. Inside, he found a stack of sandwiches. 'Something strange is going on around here,' Anthony said before taking a big bite.

'**L**ook!' Murray exclaimed. 'Someone put a new ending
on the song I was working on when I fell asleep.
It's pretty good.'

Murray sang the tune. The other Wiggles listened.

Jeff said, 'I like the new ending better.'

Murray smiled, 'So do I!'

Greg wasn't as pleased. His old bunny slippers were missing. 'I can't find them anywhere!' Greg cried, looking under the couch.

'They were really old slippers,' Murray pointed out.

'Maybe they just couldn't stand your feet any longer,' Anthony teased.

Greg shook his head. 'Even bunny slippers don't just hop away.'

Anthony started pacing back and forth. 'Someone is definitely doing strange things in this house, but I'm afraid we're too tired to stay up all night to find out who, how, and why.'

'If only we had a watchdog,' Murray said.

'I know!' said Greg. 'Maybe we can just ask our pal Wags to be our watchdog.'

So The Wiggles went to Wags' house to ask if he would stay at their house to clear up the mystery.

Wags agreed. He was always happy to help his friends.

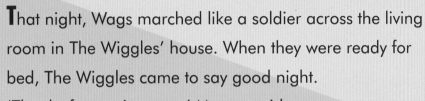

That night, Wags marched like a soldier across the living room in The Wiggles' house. When they were ready for bed, The Wiggles came to say good night.

'Thanks for staying over,' Murray said.

'I feel better knowing that you're here,' Anthony added.

'It's nice to have a dog around the house,' Jeff agreed.

Then The Wiggles went to bed.

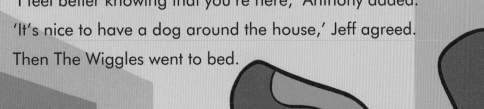

The Wiggles were soon fast asleep. Later, Anthony, Greg, and Murray woke to the sound of barking.
'Woof! WOOF!' Wags pointed to Jeff.
The fourth Wiggle was sound asleep—but walking around wearing Greg's magic hat and eating Anthony's raisins!

'**H**e's sleepwalking! Anthony exclaimed.

Just then, Jeff finished the raisins, took off the magic hat, and started walking back to his bedroom.

'He seems to be going back to bed,' Greg whispered.
Murray yawned. 'Maybe we should go back to bed, too.'
Anthony agreed. 'Yes, we'll figure this out tomorrow.'

The next morning, with the wiggly mystery solved, Jeff was amazed by what the other Wiggles told him. 'Being tired can do strange things to people,' Murray explained. 'With all the singing, travelling, cooking, and cleaning, we haven't been getting enough rest. I think what we all need is a good night's sleep.'

'That's it, then!' exclaimed Greg. 'We'll divide up the chores around the house and plan our rehearsals and concerts so that we can always get a good night's sleep.' 'And we can keep the schedule in the kitchen so that we can always look at it to remind us,' suggested Anthony. 'Well, if it's in the kitchen,' Murray whispered to Greg, 'we know that Anthony will always be reminded!'

The Wiggles were all very pleased with this solution and were looking forward to a good night's sleep.
They couldn't be sure that Jeff wouldn't sleepwalk again, but they had one last plan to make sure that they would hear him if he started to walk around the house ...

... they tied bells to Jeff's slippers!

THE END